Wild KNIGHTS OF HEAT

Hot Gay Erotica

ANGUS MACGREGOR

Please feel free to send me an email. Just know that these emails are filtered by my publisher. Good news is always welcome.

Angus MacGregor - **angus_macgregor@awesomeauthors.org**

You might also want to check my blog for Updates and interesting info. angus-macgregor.awesomeauthors.org

About the Publisher

4Fun Publishing, a member of **BLVNP Incorporated**, 340 S. Lemon #6200, Walnut CA 91789, info@blvnp.com / legal@blvnp.com
NOTE: Due to the highly emotional reaction of some people to works of erotic fiction, any email sent to the above address that contains foul language or religious references is automatically deleted by our anti-spam software and will not be seen. All other communications are welcome.

DISCLAIMER

Please don't be stupid and kill yourself. This book is a work of FICTION. Do not try any new sexual practice that you find in this book. It is fiction and not to be confused with reality. Neither the author nor the publisher or its associates assume any responsibility for any loss, injury, death or legal consequences resulting from acting on the contents in this book. Every character in this book is over 18 years of age. The author's opinions are not to be construed as the opinions of the publisher. The material in this book is for entertainment purposes ONLY. Enjoy.

Hart Mountain Hotshots Book 6

Wild Knights of Heat

Hot Gay Erotica

By: Angus MacGregor

© **Angus MacGregor 2014**
ISBN: 978-1-62761-980-6

The alarm jarred Tom from a deep sleep. His hand was tucked inside his underwear gripping hard around his penis which was rock hard with morning wood. He pulled his hand out and slapped the phone to silence the alarm. He pushed the covers back and slid the elastic of his briefs down underneath his loose sack and enjoyed the breeze from the fan blowing on his sensitive shaft. His thick, loose foreskin fell back and revealed the brick red glans that shimmered with early morning precum. He gripped the flesh and tucked an arm under his head and watched the tip disappear inside the sheath of skin, tickling and tantalizing his desire. He slid his hand down and adjusted the thick chrome cock ring that circled his thick member and scrotum. The soft dark brown hairs flared out around it like a Christmas wreath. His balls were full and filled his loose sack. It had been three days since he had unloaded his sperm and he could feel the pressure and burn in his groin. He ran his large, calloused hands across his hairy chest. He brushed across his nipples and felt them harden then slid down to grip his cock again, sliding it briskly up and down until it stood straight up.

He grinned. It might take a cock ring these days, but his penis was still very cooperative. He knew plenty of other fifty year old guys who needed blue pills and a touch of Jesus to keep their pecker up these days. Too much mileage on the body along with smoke and bad food took its toll on many. Tom had staved off some of the ravages of time with hard work and exercise and a good deal of sex. God, he loved sex. Always had it seemed. His biceps still bulged with veins and he could dig fire line all day alongside his rookies and they would give out before him all the time. He had been working these fires for 32 years. He had dodge the bullet more times than he could count. It was sobering to think of the men and boys he had worked with that were no longer around. Wildfire was a heartless bitch for sure. A lump raised in his throat thinking of Jason Patterson and young Caleb Johannsen. Tom had loved them both so much. Jason was closer than any brother. He had spent so many hours working and playing with him. He smiled thinking of his meaty backside covered with blond fur that he had such an intimate knowledge of. And Caleb, so young and tender. The smoothness of his belly and ass against Tom's furry bearded face and the sweetness of his boyhole that parted so easily when his cock pressed against it. It was hard to believe he had been a virgin when Tom entered him for the first time.

But that was in the past now and this current crop of rookies showed some interesting promise as well, especially Ian. Tom had felt an instant attraction to the solid farm boy and thankfully, it seemed Ian felt comfortable around him as well. Over the years, some of the rookies just didn't connect with an older hippie looking guy with a long ponytail and beard. But then the boys like Ian or Caleb made up for it. The daddy-son thing was a strong bond for some of these young guys. Tom liked what he saw from Jason Patterson's boy, Jesse too. God, the boy looked so much like Jason it was frightening. That little friend of his, Brandon, was a hard-worker too. And even though he was a wiseass, he found the young guy smart and sexy as hell. The other boys were still somewhat of an enigma, but the summer was just getting started and he would have a chance to work with all of them. With any luck, his cock would be well acquainted with them as well.

Tom looked back at his phone and cursed, pushing his big frame off the bed and plodding toward the shower. He turned the water on and stepped underneath the new rain showerhead Ben and Colton had helped him install. He had to admit, it was wonderful. Soft and gentle, the showerhead poured water over his 6 foot 2 inch frame, over his sturdy shoulders and down his strong back to his round ass cheeks that were still firm even though gravity was cruel and tried so hard to cause his firm rounded butt cheeks to sag or shrivel to old man ass. But so far, his hard work and exercise was keeping most of that away, even if the wrinkles and grey hairs still kept coming. He soaped up his thick matted armpits and moved down his furry chest and belly to his cock. He soaped it generously and eased the cock ring off his shaft and balls, sliding it into the soap dish. He had become so accustomed to wearing the heavy chrome ring, his dick felt light and weightless without it. He soaped his fingers and dug them deep inside his furry hole. His eyes closed as he fingered his prostate. He stuffed three fat fingers into his stretched hole and pumped them in and out of his anus until it tingled and throbbed. His cock was rigid now and he felt the need to piss.

Tom stepped out of the flow of the shower and laid his back against the cool tile. He took his penis and slid his foreskin all the way back and exhaled, sending a thick yellow stream of piss up to his chest and then to his face and lips. He opened his mouth and allowed the warm salty flow to fill his mouth. He tried to remember exactly when he started loving piss and figured it must have been with Jason. He smiled thinking of how many times he had been on his knees between those furry blond legs while Jason's fire hose showered him with clear clean pee. That had been their secret for so long. But recently, he had wondered if some of the new rookies might be open to the idea with him. He knew it was a little kinky, but by today's standards when guys walked around with clothespins on their nipples or pierced their scrotum or even put a big thick PA through their glans, he figured it was pretty mild. His piss continued to fill his mouth and dribble down his beard and onto his furry chest, tickling his belly and penis as it trailed off to the shower floor. When he finished, he stood back under the shower and resoaped his body and then washed his long hair and beard.

Tom absentmindedly ran his left thumb over his ring finger. He was still getting used to the idea of being divorced. After more than 25 years, his wife had found another man. No doubt, all those months away on fires didn't help. They had been happy together and even now, parted on mostly good terms. Paula was still nearby with her new husband; ten years younger, a college man, with a shaved head and chest. Maybe after all the years, Paula had gotten tired of the hair along with Tom's long hours and not-so-secret sexual connections with members of the crew. Paula had known about the hotshots from the time she and Tom had married. He laid it out for her before they said their vows, making it clear that she would be the only woman in his life. But his brothers…they would always come first and yes, he would routinely be fucking them. She had been more intrigued than horrified. She found Tom to be a sweet and attentive lover. He was a creative, gentle lover that never failed to make her cum. He had given her two daughters that he adored. She had asked him once if he was sorry they had not had a boy. He had smiled and reminded her he had dozens of sons, all of whom he was utterly devoted to. More than ten of the boys had lived at their home over the last thirty years from a few weeks to two years. Those had been the very best times for Tom. He didn't even have to leave home to satiate his desires during those times. But he also wondered if those times had added up to finally be the final straw for Paula.

As he slid the heavy cock ring back around his genitals, he recalled coming home early two years ago to find Paula and her new beau in bed together. He heard the moans and moved quietly in the hall and opened the bedroom door enough to watch Paula hungrily sucking the smooth man's large penis. His mushroom head glistened with her saliva as he pumped in and out of her eager mouth, breasts jostling back and forth. Her pussy was wet and open as she bent forward sucking him, the inner folds swollen and pink. He felt his cock harden as he remembered the man pulling his penis from her mouth and mount her from behind as he always did. But he soon pulled her back so they were on their sides, his massive cock pumping in and out of her bushy vagina, deep and hard, holding her big breasts as he continued to thrust. He came in loud, low grunts, filling her pussy with so much sperm it leaked out the sides and down her legs. As sad as Tom had been to realize what this meant, he honestly was glad Paula had a lover that knew how to fuck. Part of him even wished he could be on the receiving end of that magnificent cock.

But even though he missed the company of being married, if he was honest, he was enjoying being single again. He had just finished up a year with one of the rookies. Cory had lived with him all of last year while he attended the Oregon State University. The small twenty-year-old had been a great companion and even better lover. After the first month, Cory had moved into Tom's room and bed and the two of them had lived as married men for the most part. Interestingly, Cory was engaged to a girl attending George Fox University in Newberg. Madeline was sweet and pretty, but was determined to be a virgin when she married. So Cory was the devoted fiancé who never pressured Madeline for more than the occasional hand job when they made out. He would come back from those dates and fuck the ever-loving shit out of Tom, much to the big man's delight. Tom attended his wedding and actually shed tears mourning the loss of his FWB, but was happy the two kids were together. He figured Madeline would be pregnant in a few months knowing how much Cory loved to fuck and how much cum the boy had in those big balls of his.

Tom finished dressing and made a healthy breakfast that he ate while he read the newspaper. He was surprised to hear a knock on the door a few minutes later. He looked at his phone: 7:32 AM. *Who could this be this early* he thought heading for the door. He opened it to find two of the Hart Mountain rookies standing on his porch looking nervous.

"Hey fellas. What brings you around so early?" Tom asked.

Ian Lander smiled and shrugged his shoulders. "Hi Tom, uh, can we come in for a minute? Just need to talk." The solid farm boy smiled weakly, his mahogany brown eyes shining in the early morning sun.

"Sure, sounds interesting. Come on in. How's it hanging there, Aaron?" Tom said to the other rookie.

"Heavy and to the right," Aaron said laying a hand on Tom's shoulder. Tom laughed.

The rookies came into the kitchen and sat at the table, reaching over and grabbing some toast left on the plate along with a banana and the leftover sausages.

"Hey, I was going to take that for my lunch today," Tom said with mock annoyance. The young guys froze with mouths full of food until Tom broke out laughing. "Not to worry. But you could have asked, jackasses."

"Sorry, Tom. Just pretty hungry this morning," Ian said swallowing. Tom slid the pitcher of orange juice over with a couple of empty coffee mugs and the boys poured themselves some juice and drained the cups.

"So what was so important you slugs got out of bed so early?"

Ian and Aaron looked at one another. "We kind of got kicked out of our apartment," Aaron said meekly.

"What?" Tom asked

Ian began. "It was stupid. We were at the stupid Harriet's Marriet boarding house. She ought to be fined for that name alone," Ian started. "It's not even spelled right and it doesn't rhyme."

"Never mind that. What happened?"

"Well, see, I was just paying for me to stay there. The landlady got really mad when she figured out that Aaron was living there too. I told her we would pay the difference and everything, but she just turned into a raving bitch and told us to get out," Ian said.

"I think she might have spied on us or something. The way she was so mad and looking at us weird," Aaron added.

"Spied on you? What were you boys doing?"

"Nothing. I mean, it's a small place, you know? There's just one double bed so I guess she knew we were sharing it. "

Tom smiled. "You boys get a bit loud with the fun times?"

Ian's face reddened and Aaron looked down. "Maybe," Ian said.

Tom looked up at the clock. "Well, it's about time to head off to work. Why don't you fellas just plan on coming back here tonight and we can talk and make a plan."

"We can pay, Tom, to stay here for a while," Ian added hopefully.

"Oh I'm sure there are some things you can do around here to pay your way," Tom added with a grin. Ian's face grew red again.

Tom grabbed his gear and headed out to his truck telling the guys to just jump in with him.

"It's silly to drive two rigs to work. Save your gas," he said.

The three men sat in the cab. Aaron sat in the middle and his big leg rested close to Tom's as they rolled down the driveway and out onto the street. With his legs that were spread wide, Tom noticed and a sturdy bulge filled his Nomex pants. Tom let his leg rest against Aaron's knee and enjoyed the young man pressing back against his leg. His cock swelled and the study chrome ring kept his erection solid and clearly visible down the leg of his pants. Tom saw Aaron's eyes continue to dart to the left and widen as they saw the big member straining against the Kevlar fabric. Tom reached down and casually scratched his balls and let his hand rub his hard prick until the head pushed tight and made a large mound in his right pocket.

"Hey Aaron, can you reach in my pocket and grab my phone," Tom said shifting in his seat and clearly making his right-hand pants pocket accessible. The young man looked at him with a sly smile and slid his thick fingers into Tom's pocket fishing for his phone, making sure to slide his hand around the man's straining erection as he did. He handed the phone to Tom.

"Thanks, buddy," the man said reaching over to rub Aaron's inner thigh dangerously close to his crotch.

Ian laughed. "Tom's got the magic touch, Aaron. Better watch out," the rookie said with a knowing chuckle.

The men pulled into the parking lot and made their way to the crew house with the other members of the hotshots, fist-bumps and pats on the back greeting them as they gathered around the tables for early morning briefing after clocking in. Tom's gaze moved around the group taking in the crew and assessing how this cadre stacked up with all of the other crews he had worked with. He smiled seeing young Jesse

Patterson's hand draped casually around Brandon's shoulders while the smaller man's hand rested comfortably in Jesse's lap. Ben sat on a stool with Colton on a stool behind him, his big legs wrapping around Ben's meaty ones like a two-man bobsled team. Rick sat near Eric, their shoulders touching, much like Chad and Bayard. Tom smiled seeing how much genuine love and affection there was on display in his group. These men meant everything to him and it was heartwarming to see how important they were to one another. He could close his eyes and see almost every one of them naked. He had fucked almost all of them and by the end of the summer, he had no doubt it would be one-hundred percent. He had lost count of how many brothers he had slid inside of over the years, hundreds most likely. As Jake went through the weather and likely deployments that may be coming up, his mind wandered.

Growing up in rural Maryland, Tom's first brush with intimacy with another guy during his senior year who had come with a schoolmate and fellow Boy Scout. Tom had grown up with two older sisters and a kind but emotionally distant father. His good friend, Charlie, lived less than a mile away from him and the two shared the responsibilities and experiences of rural farm boys. They were in the same class and shared interests like fishing and camping. As Jake continued, Tom's mind settled back to that steamy summer evening at some Boy Scout camporee when they were councilors, sharing the small two-man tent with Charlie.

"Goddamn, it's so hot my eyeballs are sweating," Charlie had said crawling into the tent after the campfire circle that night.

"I know," Tom said. "I'll never fall asleep at this rate."

Charlie threw his boots down at the foot of the sleeping bag and ripped off his socks. The smell of sweaty feet filled the tent.

"Holy shit. Maybe we should go take a shower before we go to sleep. It might cool us down. You think there's still time?"

"If we go right now, maybe. The dads rarely make a stink about boys actually wanting to bathe."

Ten minutes later, the boys stood beside one another in the cool water of the bath house. They were alone there other than two older high school aged scouts who paid them no attention at all. Tom recalled how he continued to look sideways at Charlie's naked ass shining white in the dim light of the showers, dark tanned legs and back in sharp contrast. When Charlie turned around, his dick was half hard and framed with a thick brown bush of fur. Tom instantly had felt relieved. Since he had started growing pubic hair, he wasn't completely sure other boys looked the same. Charlie saw him staring and smiled.

"Your dick is even more hairy than mine. That's cool. You should see my older brother's. It's like a horse or something." Tom laughed with him.

The boys got out of the shower and slid shorts on and ran back to the tent without drying off, feeling the drops bead on their skin. They flopped into the tent breathless, laying back on top of their sleeping bags. Charlie reached down and unfastened his shorts and slid them off laying naked on top of his bag. Tom remember how the drops of water on his chest and eyelashes reflected the moonlight from outside.

"It's too hot to sleep with clothes," Charlie said, clearly indicating he didn't want to be the only one naked. Tom fumbled with his shorts and lay back feeling the air swirl around his balls and stiffen his penis.

"Your dick looks different than mine," Charlie had said, indicating his circumcised mushroom head.

Tom slid his loose foreskin down and exposed the damp tip of his uncut penis, swelling hard in the sweltering tent.

"Yeah. Mine wasn't cut by the doctor when I was born. Neither was my dad's, but I hardly ever get to see his."

"I see my dad's sometimes. It's big for sure, like my brother's. That's cool the way the skin slides up like that," Charlie said watching Tom nonchalantly stroking his penis.

"You can touch it if you want," Tom said hoping Charlie did want to.

Charlie's warm hard slid around his shaft and began to side it up and down. The feeling was electric and Tom's cock became rock hard in seconds. "Wow, your dick gets really big. It feels really cool to jack. Can you jack mine?"

Tom reached over and gripped his friend's erection and slid his hand up and down the boy's shaft, enjoying the feeling of the sliding skin and the damp, sticky fluid that oozed from the tip just like his did. Tom remembered standing up on his knees belly to belly with Charlie as they held their dicks together while Tom slid his foreskin back and forth over both of their dick heads, the precum making it slick and juicy in his hands. Tom could feel Charlie's breath on his face, his dark fuzz mustache wet with sweat. Tom had closed his eyes as Charlie's lips touched his, his mouth opening slightly as the boy's tongue parted his lips and moved inside his mouth causing his cock to erupt in hot spams over his sticky fingers. A gasp let him know Charlie was cumming too, more sperm flowing into his hand as Tom continued to stroke their connected cocks.

"You cum so much," Charlie whispered.

An hour later, Tom had reached over to grip Charlie's penis again. The boy returned the gesture and they stroked one another until they were hard again. Then Charlie repositioned himself and Tom gasped as his dick slid inside his friend's warm mouth. Tom pumped in and out of Charlie's hungry mouth, spreading his legs wide as the boy explored his balls and hole with his hands. Finally, Tom spun around and latched on Charlie's stiff prick and began to suck as he felt Charlie doing with him. He pulled the boy's flat belly to his face, his soft pubes tickling his nose. He felt Charlie's penis swell and fill his mouth with salty semen, pumping in and out deep within his mouth. Charlie had lain on his arm after that, his soft lips touching own again, this time flavored with cum.

"Keep this secret, but let's keep doing it," he had whispered. Tom had nodded and kissed him again.

Two nights later after another shower just before lights out, the two boys sucked and ground their dicks deep into one another's mouths, licking and sucking one another with abandon. Charlie had broken off the sucking and pushed Tom onto his belly and crawled between his legs, pulling his butt cheeks apart and spitting on his hole, rubbing his fingers into Tom's fuzzy anus until the knobby muscle relaxed and allowed the boy's thick finger to slide inside. Tom spread his legs wide as Charlie licked and sucked on his sack while working his hole with his finger. Soon, the boy positioned himself between Tom's legs, resting the head of his penis on his soggy hole.

"Relax and push out a little like you are taking a dump," Charlie whispered in his ear. A moment later, the boy's cock pushed past his ass ring, pain shooting through Tom's belly. Charlie held back and whispered for him to relax again, pushing in and out in small rocking motions until his belly resting against Tom's butt, his penis balls deep inside him.

"I'm going to fuck you now," he whispered as he slid his dick back and then back down inside his ass. Soon, the tent was filled with slapping sounds of skin on skin, Charlie's balls banging hard against Tom's bigger set. Tom spread his legs as wide as possible as Charlie fucked deep and hard into his virgin hole, groaning loudly as his seed flowed into his stretched hole. Charlie collapsed on Tom's back, breathing deeply as his dick slid out of Tom's spent anus.

"Now you do it to me," Charlie had ordered rolling off Tom and onto his belly. Tom followed the steps he had just experienced, even going so far as sliding his tongue inside Charlie's clean butt crack. Charlie had groaned into his pillow as Tom penetrated his ass, burying himself deep inside the boy's hole and plowing him again and again until he released his nutt inside his friend.

The next evening as they showered, this time alone in the bath house, Charlie had sunk to his knees and sucked on Tom, pulling him deep inside his mouth. When Tom pulled back commenting that he really had to piss, Charlie gripped his dick and looked at him with a wicked grin.

"So go ahead."

Tom stared and looked around, but then relaxed as his pee flowed out in a warm stream of yellow, bathing Charlie's chest, belly, and dick. Charlie stood up and pushed Tom down to his knees.

"I want to pee on you now."

Tom stared as Charlie's penis swelled and a warm stream of urine flowed onto his chest and belly and down to his hard dick. Without thinking, he gripped the boy's dick and directed the flow to his face. He opened his mouth and let the tangy warmth of Charlie's piss fill his mouth. He swallowed the liquid then began to suck Charlie's cock while the boy pumped in and out of his mouth. They broke apart and soaped one another up and ran back to the tent wearing their towels, giggling the whole way.

And for the next few years, whenever they had a sleepover, a campout, or just the odd Sunday afternoon hike, they continued to fuck like bunnies even as they began to discover girls and eventually, fall in love with them. The sweetness and passion of those early memories flooded over him, swelling his cock to a rock hard tent pole.

"Hey, Tom. You with me?" Jake said, clearly asking him a question that he had no idea of the answer.

"What's that?" The crew broke into laughter.

"I was giving out assignments for today. You need to take west patrol. Pick a couple of rooks to go along with you in Engine 41," Jake said shaking his head.

Tom looked up and noticed all the rookies had their heads down hoping not to be picked. He was used to this. He had a clear reputation for not only being a stickler for the rules but a bull top that loved breaking rookies in. He looked at Brandon and Jesse then over to Nick and Jordan. But decided to let his morning guests get the benefit of his veteran expertise.

"I'll take Ian and Aaron today," he said. Several of the guys chuckled and nodded.

"Better hold on to your cornhole, boys," Bayard added with a laugh.

The engine wound its way up the rutted forest road toward a landing in a clearcut that looked out on the west slopes of Mary's Peak. Aaron and Ian sat in the middle and passenger seats while Tom drove. They had driven in total silence for miles. The rookies couldn't tell if Tom was mad or daydreaming or what. Ian kept looking over at the big man, his pony tail blowing in the wind coming in from the open window. He absentmindedly continued to rub his hand on his crotch as he drove. The morning was bright, the sky beginning to turn from blue to the dull washed out white of summer in Oregon when the sky filled with dust and smoke from fires. Finally, Ian couldn't stand the silence any more.

"Um, everything okay there, Tom," he asked.

Tom shook his head out of his reverie. He was still enjoying thinking about his fun times with Charlie for some reason this morning and seemed oblivious to almost everything else.

"What? Oh yeah. Guess I just have my mind on other things today." He looked over at the inquisitive looks on the rookies. "Relax fellas. I don't know what you are expecting, but I probably won't rape you until after lunch." Tom reached into the back of the truck's rear seat and brought back some water bottles out of the cooler.

"Drink up, boys. Gotta stay hydrated." Tom opened the bottle and downed almost the entire contents, letting the water run out the corners of his mouth and down into his thick beard.

"Hey Tom," Aaron began. "How long have you been growing your beard?"

"Hmm, well I've had this long beard since 1978 or something like that. I have trimmed it a ton of times. Cut my hair as well, but I'm a hairy fucker, always have been. It just keeps growing. Back when I was a kid, I heard someone say they had grown their hair out to make room for their brain. That sounded like a pretty good strategy to me."

The guys laughed. Ian was in the middle seat now and he let his hand casually rest on Tom's thigh. Tom took his hand and moved it to his crotch.

"You've been staring at my junk all day, Ian. It's okay if you want to hold it while I'm driving. Not like it's the first time." Tom referred to the night back in fire school when he and Ian had shared a tent. He had also shared some of his patented pot cookies and spent two hours exploring the rookie's tight furry boyhole and thick cut dick, welcoming him into the brotherhood with long, deep thrusts from his cock. It had been like a dance rehearsed many times before. The partner had changed, but the enjoyment and dance steps remained the same. Ian's warm hand gripped Tom's semi-hard erection and slid back and forth against the Nomex fabric.

"That was a pretty fun week, Tom. You taught me a lot, that's for sure. I was totally freaked out being your partner and everyone kept giving me a hard time, but you were cool. And you stretched my ass out pretty good too," Ian said with a grin.

"I take it you and Aaron have been practicing with one another since then?"

Ian's cheeks blushed. Aaron's hand slid into the sandy haired boy's lap and fondled with his balls.

"You could say that," Aaron said. "He's a pretty great teacher too."

"So tell me how you boys hooked up," Tom said, truly interested as he enjoyed Ian exploring his crotch.

Aaron spoke up quickly telling the story of his fire school week and his experiences with Jake, his first with a man. He told about sharing his boyhood stories with the other rookies and how he had been a virgin when Jake took him during fire school.

"Just like Tom did with me," Ian said continuing to rub the man's cock through his pants.

Aaron continued his story. "Anyway, the guys were kind of joking but sort of suggested we hang out and see if we had some chemistry or something since all the other rooks had mostly paired up. So, we sort of did. Ian invited me to come stay with him in his room at the boarding house since I knew my folks would be all weird about us sharing my room at home. I was looking for a way to get out of the house anyway."

Ian picked up the story. "That first night we stayed up late and played PS3 and drank a few beers and smoke a little weed. We got tired and when it was time to sleep, I remember this doofus just standing in the middle of the room looking around trying to figure out what to do. I could tell he didn't want to just climb into bed with me and was looking at my chair thinking he could sleep there. I finally just scooted over to the far side of my bed and said "Get in, you idiot.'"

Aaron laughed. "It was just funny, you know. I laid down beside him and Ian here just rolled over toward the wall and fell asleep. I laid there with my ass bumped up against his for a while, listening to him fall asleep and start to snore. I turned over and sort of spooned him and fell asleep."

"I woke up with this goob all wrapped around me, hugging me tight. Felt pretty good, I had to admit. I could feel his hairy belly against my back and feel his boner pressing against my butt. I just wiggled around until it fit into my crack and fell back asleep. Woke up in the morning with his guy's face right against mine. I reached up and touched his face, feeling his scratchy cheeks and lips."

"Which woke me up. It was very odd to wake up and have this guy's big meaty face right there an inch from mine. But it also felt really nice. His hand sort of disappeared and then I felt it wrapped around my morning wood, so I just did the same, staring into damn baby blues of his. And the next thing, I just wanted his dick in my mouth, so I just climbed under the covers and pulled out his schlong and swallowed it all the way to his short and curlies."

Ian reached his other hand over and slid it into Aaron's lap and gripped his cock. "And he sucked me good, stroking the shaft and gobbling my knob and bathing my balls and when I got ready to come, he just nursed my dick like a starving calf and swallowed every drop of my pecker paste."

"And Ian pulled me up and planted this big kiss on my lips, tasting his nutt on my tongue, which was super hot. He pushed me back and pulled my shorts down underneath my sack and starting sucking me. I think I lasted about thirty seconds before I was shooting my wad down his throat," Aaron said with a smile.

"Since then, we pretty much been doing the same thing every day. Sometimes two or three times a day," Ian said. "I can't get enough of his lug's dick."

Tom pulled over into a spur of the forest road and turned the engine off. "That sounds great, fellas. Glad to hear you are enjoying spending time together. I knew Ian here was a loveable guy. Good to hear you are too, Aaron. Might as well have our lunch out here. Grab your cooler and let's take a short hike."

The rookies followed Tom into the forest that lay thick and green against the road. The trail he moved on was barely recognizable, but soon they walked into a clearing and stood before a double waterfall that roared out of the rocks fifty feet above. The men stood looking at the cascade of crystal clean water, bending their heads back to see the top of the falls.

"I didn't know this was here," Aaron said in almost a whisper.

"Me either."

"It's called Yaquina Falls and it's a pretty well-kept secret. This used to be private land but the State of Oregon owns it now. It isn't developed or anything. It's written up in a few hiking guides, but only a few find it. I've seen a few hikers here, mostly college boys. Nice place to have a lunch and a dip in the pool. Here, keep drinking water guys," Tom said handing more water bottles around.

Soon, the guys were settled down on the ground eating their lunches, watching the falls, and talking about fire and fucking.

"So, are you boys taking it up the shitter from one another?" Tom asked munching on some pretzels.

Ian looked over at Aaron. "Um, sort of haven't gotten there yet."

"Real close a few times. I've woke up with his guy's dick head up my crack pretty far."

"Any reason you are waiting?" Tom asked

"Not really. Just haven't taken the plunge. Guess we keep waiting for the other guy to take the lead," Ian said.

"Well, fucking isn't always for everyone. But from what I remember, Ian, you were a natural. You seemed to take my cock nice and easy during fire school."

Ian laughed. "There wasn't anything nice and easy about it. You plowed my virgin hole hard, Tom. But at least you used lots of lube and took your time sliding inside me before you turned on the jackhammer."

"Sounds like Jake. My bobbum was stretched out like a cheap whore by the end of that week," Aaron said. "But it was fun too." The men sat quietly and listened to the water and finished their lunches. "Um, we gonna be on the receiving end of your big dick today?"

"Well, you never know. It's still quite a while before we end the shift. And then you boys are headed home with me tonight too."

Ian stood up and faked gripping his ample backside. "I have a feeling my boy hole is going to be barking pretty good by tonight," he joked.

Tom smiled. "And I'm thinking that would please both you boys pretty good." They smiled and gave one another knowing looks.

"Damn, I need to take a piss," Aaron said. "All that water and listening to this damn waterfall is about to make me wet myself."

"Me too," Ian said closing up his lunch cooler and looking around for a good tree to pee on.

"I don't want either of you taking a leak. Not yet," Tom said with authority. The rookies looked over at him in surprise. He was bending down unlacing his boots.

"I really have to go, Tom. It'll just take a minute," Ian said.

"Rookie, you take another step and I will write you up and you'll be sitting home all summer long," Tom said pulling his shirt tail out of his pants and then bending to remove his socks. The rookies stared at the man and then back at each other.

"Hey, what's going on Tom? Are you okay?" Aaron asked moving his hand to grip his penis and hold on for dear life. Tom pulled his shirt and t-shirt off and then unbuckled his belt and stepped out of his pants. Then with a quick tug, he pushed his briefs down and stepped out of them, his semi-hard dick hanging heavy in the chrome ring.

"You want to fuck us right now?" Ian asked timidly feeling his sphincter contract.

Tom looked at the rookies shaking in their boots. "Okay fellas, strip. Be quick about it too."

Aaron and Ian looked at one another and mutely began to unlace their boots. A moment, later the two rookies tossed their underwear on top of their gear and stood in the cool shade feeling the breeze flow between their legs and around their nutsack. They held their hands in front of their privates and shifted nervously from foot to foot. Tom dropped to his knees in the green mossy ground beckoning the young men forward. Tom pushed their hands away from their dicks to reveal two hard cocks pointing in his face. He looked into their eyes where a mixture of confusion, apprehension, and desire met. He lightly gripped their full, furry nutsacks and pulled them gently toward him.

"You boys still need to piss?" Tom asked. They nodded in sync with one another. "Well, you better go ahead then," Tom said moving his hands to their rigid cocks, pointing them toward his face and chest. The rookies' eyes flew open wider with realization dawning.

"You want us to pee on you?" Ian asked incredulously.

"Really?" Aaron added.

"Let 'em flow, fellas. Don't overthink it. Just relax."

The young men looked at one another and relaxed their muscles and felt their piss flow from their hard dicks. It sprayed out like a fire hose onto Tom's furry chest and into his long beard. He guided the flow on to his belly and down to his cock ring circled penis, hard and stiff in the breeze. Then he opened his mouth and directed the flow into his mouth where it bubbled, filling his throat until he gulped and swallowed and then allowed the flow to fill him again. Ian reached over and slid his arm around Aaron's waist. Aaron did the same, letting his hand slid down and rest on Ian's meaty ass. The rookies stared in wide-eyed wonder as the older man hungrily lapped up their pee and then moved forward and began to suck them. The boys stood close and fit their cocks in tandem into Tom's skilled mouth. His hands gripped their butts and fingers slid into their cracks, pressing against their holes until he penetrated them with thick probes. He moved to their balls and sucked and licked the full sacks until their scrotum's dripped with saliva. The young guys' bellies were close and touching as he continued to suck them. Ian looked at Aaron and pulled this scruffy-faced guy toward him, their lips touching. Soon, their mouths were open as they kissed and darted their tongues around one another's mouth.

Tom pulled back and stood up. "Oh your knees, boys." The two obeyed, sinking to their knees, looking up as Tom and his large cock hovered above them. Tom sighed and a big fat clear yellow flow of piss streamed from his dick and began to spray across their chests and nipples, down to their bellies and dicks and then up to their faces. The rookies turned their faces and pulled back, but Tom's hard spraying dick shot across their chins and lips and blasted its way into their lips that were pressed tightly together.

"Open up, fellas. That's a direct order."

The rookies closed their eyes and felt the tangy, warm fluid to fill their mouths and splash their faces. Soon, the flow stopped and they looked up at Tom, allowing the urine to flow out of their mouths and down their chests. Their cocks were rock hard, dripping with precum. Their chests were beaded with piss, dripping off their face, their belly, and erections. The rookies watched Tom rise and walk toward the rock-lined pool the falls crashed into and step down into the clear water and slide underneath he rippling surface. He stayed under for almost twenty seconds before spluttering to the top.

"You fellas gonna sit in the engine wearing my piss all afternoon or are you gonna wash off?"

Ian and Aaron gingerly stepped toward the pool and carefully stepped around the rocks and sucked in their breath. The water was like ice. But they kept moving into it and soon floated beside Tom.

"Nice, huh?" he asked. The rookies shook their heads. "First time?" he asked.

The young guys nodded again. "I never did the pee thing before," Ian said.

"I was talking about swimming in a waterfall pool," Tom said with a grin.

"Oh. Yeah, this is new too."

Tom glanced at his wristwatch. "Better get on the road again, boys. I got a feeling we will be fightin' fire before we head home today."

Tom rose from the pool and began to shake the water off his body like a big shaggy dog before sliding his clothes back on. The rookies made their way out of the pool and followed suit, pulling their fire clothes on over their wet bodies and then climbing back in the engine. True to his prediction, a smoke column was spotted in the Lobster Valley area later in the day and the crew along with most of the other hotshots arrived to work on the operator caused fire that grew to five acres before they caught it. Inmate crews from the local prison camp were ordered to work the fire mop-up for the night. The crew made their way back to the compound around 7:00 PM and stood under the showers with the other firefighters, washing away the soot and grime of the day.

Tom glanced around the steamy room and enjoyed the collection of naked men, soaping and washing together. He saw Jesse's hand casually slide inside Brandon's tight butt crack briefly as they stood close together. Across the room, he watched Eric and Chad wash off each other's backs and asses, Eric's cock hard, the tip casually brushing against Chad's furry butt. Sam was sharing a shower pole with Jordan and Nick and was actually slowly stroking their erect cocks as they all stood under the water. Normally, the crew kept the PDA to a minimum in the showers, never knowing who might be around. But tonight, it seemed to Tom, most were throwing caution to the wind. Ian and Aaron stood around the shower pole with him. The rookies were chatting in whispers with one another, turning to wash one another's backs. Aaron's hands parted Ian's butt and slid up and down the young man's crack slowly as they spoke. Tom let his cock ring slide from his balls and dick. He hung it on the water handle and watched the young guys flirt and touch one another.

His mind drifted back to his first summer with Hart Mountain. He was so young. The seventies were almost over and the eighties were on the way. There were no fire schools or even much preparatory training back then. You showed up and the next thing you knew, you were holding a hose or digging fireline, with a veteran firefighter assigned to mentor you. His first day on the job, the crew boss, Steve had driven him around the district, talked with him about the job, showed him how to operate the pump and various controls on the engines. In the late afternoon, he had pulled over on a forest road spur to take a leak. Tom remembered the man's hand reaching over to grip his penis and stroke it as Tom pissed. With an understanding look, Tom sunk to his knees and took the man's large uncut dick into his mouth and began to suck him. Steve pumped in and out of his mouth, holding his head, pressing tight into his nose until the wild furry bush surrounding his big cock was smothering him. His jaws were stretched wide servicing the thick 8-inch penis that leaked precum by the gallon.

Minutes later, he was bend over the back of the engine, Steve's leaking cock buried deep inside his furry nineteen-year-old anus. His friend, Charlie, had fucked him plenty of times, but this was a man's cock; big, thick, and needy. The man plowed the rookie until semen flowed down his hairy legs and his asshole throbbed. It had been Steve that opened Tom's eyes to the fascination of golden showers. He spent many afternoons on patrol feeding Steve his piss or getting showered with Steve's. The man had a bladder like a horse and could soak Tom to the bone with his yellow gold. He had shown Tom where various pools and stream were easily accessible to rinse off, though sometimes, the men would return to the crew house, sticky and damp with each other's pee still ripe on the other's skin. It was visceral and manly, both humiliating and empowering at the same time. Steve taught him everything he knew about fire and fucking. Both had proven invaluable to Tom over the years.

The evening breeze had returned by the time Tom drove back toward his home, Ian and Aaron sitting beside him in the cab of his truck.

"You boys tired? Been a pretty full day," Tom said.

"Yeah, pretty beat. What's for dinner, Dad?" Ian said playfully.

Tom slid his arm around the big boy and pulled him close. "I don't know, son. What you gonna make me?"

Twenty minutes later, the men were gathered around Tom's grill cooking up some steaks. Tom had a grill basket filled with cut up onions, peppers, squash, and mushrooms. He handed cold beers around and the men joked and talked about the day. They wore shorts and undershirts and flip-flops. As the rookies manned the grill, Tom saw his neighbor, Will, was out in the backyard, looking over the fence. Will was married with a couple of daughters. Tom had gotten used to his constant voyeurism over the years. He had been playful and affectionate with many crew members over the past few years that Will and his family had lived there. Normally, Tom kept the public displays quiet, but when Will alone seemed to be out in the yard, Tom often let his hands begin to stray, watching the man stare and often rub his crotch while he observed. Tonight, Tom blatantly rubbed Ian and Aaron's big bubble butts as they cooked while chatting with Will across the fence.

"New guys on the crew?" Will asked Tom staring fixedly at Aaron and Ian bending over the grill.

"Yep. They got tossed out of their room so they are gonna be hanging with me for a while until we get on the road with out of district fires."

"They seem like good guys," Will mentioned. "Sure don't seem to mind your hands on their ass."

"Ah, you know. These young boys are freer these days than when we were young," Tom said obviously rubbing his own crotch while Will watched. "You know, you would be welcome to come over some evening and join us for some fun. I've invited you plenty of times."

Will smiled. "Maybe I will. Jesus, look at the butt on that blond kid."

"Ian. He can suck the chrome off your bumper, too."

"You are so fucking lucky," Will added. "No one's sucked my dick in two years."

"I'll take care of it tonight if you want. Shit, just jump over the fence. The boys will help out."

"I am so damn tempted. I've never tried it."

"Won't turn you gay you know. Like I tell the straight and bi rookies and vets on the crew: Just because you eat a few bananas now and then doesn't make you a monkey."

Will laughed. Tom reached over and gripped the man's cock through his shorts and watched him close his eyes and spread his legs open wider to give Tom clear access to his junk.

"Fuck, that's nice."

"So come over and play, Will."

"I'll think about it." This is what he had said a dozen times before. Tom slid his hand in the elastic waistband of his shorts and gripped the man's penis that was hard and leaking. "Jesus, that's gonna make me cum."

"Good. Feels like you need it," Tom said. The men heard a noise from Will's house and pulled apart. Moments later, Sandra poked her head out.

"Dinner, Will. Good evening, Tom."

"Good evening, Sandra. What's for dinner?"

"Spaghetti. Hurry up, Will. It's getting cold."

Will pulled back, his cock still straining hard against his shorts. "FML," he whispered with a sad smile.

"Come over later. Tell her we are watching baseball or trying to get a poker game going."

"I'll try," he said without much conviction and turned to go back inside.

Tom went back over to the grill. "You guys about ready here?"

"Yeah. Just finished up. Who's your friend there, Tom?" Ian said picking up the platter of steaks.

"Oh just Will, my neighbor."

"Man, that guy looks like he is whipped," Aaron said.

"You have no idea."

Thirty minutes later, the guys sat on Tom's couch, bellies full and heads groggy from the hard day's work and beer. Tom broke out his hookah pipe, filling it with some quality kush and the guys smoked away the cares of the day until they were relaxed and mellow. Ian had slid his shorts off and sat in his briefs, his thick cock pressing against the white cotton fabric in a conspicuous lump. Aaron got up and went to the bathroom and when he returned, he had pulled off his shirt and shorts and wore only his black American Apparel boxer briefs.

"You warm Aaron?" Tom asked staring at the young guy's meaty backside hugged tight in the cotton briefs.

"Yeah. Guess the weed got me all warmed up."

"Before you sit back down, come here a minute."

Aaron walked over to Tom. The big man reached up and slid his hand softly over Aaron's round butt cheeks and around to his sack, heavy and filling the pouch of his shorts. Tom brought his face to the boy's package and breathed deeply, inhaling the rookie's bouquet of clean musky crotch. He turned the young man around and slid his shorts down off his bubble butt and gripped a handful of meaty ass. The boy's butt was solid and smooth, with a thick trail of fur from the small triangle above his ass crack down to his manhole and around to his smoothly shaved sack. Tom pulled the mounds apart and buried his face inside the trench, kissing and licking the furry pucker of flesh. Aaron gripped his butt and pulled it further apart, pressing his ass hard against Tom's probing tongue.

"Fuck, man. That is so hot to watch," Ian said sliding his hand inside his briefs and stroking his cock.

"So get over here and eat this man's pussy," Tom ordered. Ian crawled over and turned Aaron's exposed ass and fastened his face to his friend's butt crack, licking and sucking his asshole until it was dripping and dilated. Aaron bent forward gripping the arm of the couch, his legs spread wide allowing his nutsack to hang low in midair as his friend feasted on his rosebud. He looked around seeing Tom sit back in his chair, his shorts down around his ankles, his chrome-ringed cock thick and rigid. His foreskin was pulled back and his glans leaked precum down on the leather of his chair in a long honey-like string.

Ian pressed his face as tightly against Aaron's hole as he could, his nose and mouth affixed to the boy's furry trench. Finally, he spoke through gasps of pleasure.

"Would one of you assholes please just fuck me already?"

Tom grinned and slid out of his chair and pulled Ian's shorts down and began to suck the rookie's penis until it was dripping with saliva. He grabbed a bottle of Wet and squirted a generous amount on Ian's rigid pole, shaking his hand back and forth until the shaft was totally lubed. He slid lubed fingers tenderly into Aaron's asshole while the boy moaned and gasped. With Aaron still holding on to the arm of the couch, Ian's penis slid easily into his friend's ass crack and found his smooth pucker. Ian positioned his dick head against Aaron's hole and pressed forward, just enough until Aaron sucked in his breath and pulled back.

"Relax buddy," Tom said standing up behind the back of the couch. "Suck me while Ian slips inside. Will take your mind off the process. Back and forth, nice and easy, Ian, until his pussy just lets you

Later that night, Aaron and Ian lay in bed beside one another, naked and coupled. They slowly kissed and fondled one another until their dicks were hard and leaking again. Ian rolled on his belly and grunted as Aaron's lubed cock penetrated his tight pucker. All seven inches of the boy's dick filled his ass and slammed again and again deep within his ass until Aaron moaned and sent a thick load of seed deep within Ian's manhole. Afterwards, Aaron sucked Ian, bathed his balls and even licked Ian's spent ass, tasting his nut on his hole. He blew him until Ian's sperm filled his mouth with spurts of thick creaminess.

"I could really get used to that," Aaron said, his lips only a fraction of an inch away from Ian's. The rookies could feel each other's breath against their faces, their dicks slowing draining the last of their load against each other's still heaving belly.

Earlier that night after the boys had retired to their room, Tom's phone had buzzed with a text message from Sam.

You ok if I cum over? Been a bad night for me.

Sure. Tom had answered.

The men sucked and fucked one another, hard and long, as they had so many times before. Sam's thick penis was short but beer-can thick and filled Tom's hole with surprising fullness. He had fucked Sam hard and rough afterward, filling the married man's hole with another large load of semen. Playing with the boys tonight had fueled his libido and hardened his cock to rock star status. Sam had stifled his shouts into a pillow as Tom plowed his manhole deep and hard until Sam's hole was wide and ruined. After they rested, Tom had begun again, eating his ass and then sliding 2, 3, then 4 fingers into the man's stretched anus until Sam was cumming again in silvery webs across his big furry stomach. Now in the shower, Tom knelt while Sam sprayed his piss onto Tom's chest and face, feeding him drink after drink. Tom had unleashed his own fire hose of pee into Sam's eager mouth, soaking the man's furry chest and back with light amber warmth.

They lay in one another's arms later, slowly fondling each other's penis and sacks, enjoying the slow buildup of yet another erection and cum session.

"You have any idea how many times you have fucked me?" Sam whispered feeling the steady tattoo of Tom's heart against his hand.

"No, not really."

"I figure it's got to be near two hundred or more. I must have swallowed a gallon of your nut. Way more piss too. I love you, old guy. You know that, right?"

"Yeah. I reckon I do. Remember the first time, in the showers after everyone left on that first Friday. I think you thought since you were married, you wouldn't be part of the fun."

Sam laughed. "I was probably the oldest virgin ass you ever popped."

"No, that would be ole Vince Mattiota. He was probably 52 when I deflowered his pussy. He howled almost as loud as you did."

"I knew the young guys were getting fucked pretty good. I heard them talking. But yeah, I figured I would be outside of all that. But somehow, when I was in that shower with you, seeing you stand there beside me with that fucking cock ring and hard dick, I knew you were going to rape my hole."

"Hard to rape the willing, buddy."

"Yeah, that's true. By the time you were washing my back and rubbing that big dick of yours against my ass crack, I knew I was a goner. I gripped that shower pole and you went to town on my hole. I had always heard how great a rim job was and you proved that was true. And then boom, when your cock slid into me, it was like I was being cut in half."

"And two minutes later you were reaching around to pull my ass harder and harder into your hole. You were a natural, Sammy. How are your rookies?

"Jordan and Nick, those boys love to fuck, so it's been great. Have to admit, I kind of miss the adventure of seducing a cherry pop boy. God, I remember the first time I slid inside Ben, holy Christ. So tight and that kid is fuckin' Chewbacca. It really did feel like I was the first dick ever to invade his hole, even if that might not have been the case. Now he's married like me."

"Not exactly like you," Tom chuckled. "So any news on the baby front?"

"Anne is almost ready to give up. She wants a baby so bad."

"Did you ever tell her you are shooting blanks, brother?"

"Not exactly. I just know it will kill her. "

"You have to tell her."

"I know. I've got an idea. I think she will go for it. If she does, it will be good all around. Eric and I have been talking. He's kind of in the same boat."

"How? That guy has fucking triplets."

"I know. But believe it or not, his wife is hoping for a girl. She really wants to try again. He hasn't told her his boys all dried up with that smoke inhalation he had. He's afraid to say anything. Anyway, like I said, we have a plan. "

"I think I know what you have in mind. God help you," Tom laughed. "I'm tired, Sammy. You gonna stay all night?"

"Yeah, I told Anne I had to go to work. She doesn't care. Hey, you think those boys are still awake?"

"You want more nut after all that?"

"I need to fuck a rookie tonight."

"Well, they are just down the hall. Tell them to get their asses in here."

Five minutes later, Sam's face was buried so deep in Ian's meaty ass it looked like his whole head was sliding inside. The rookie was on his belly, reaching behind to part his ass cheeks wide to let Sam have as much access as possible to his well-used hole. Sam pulled the boy's cock toward him so he could alternately suck the fat round head and Ian's smooth nutsack before drilling his hungry tongue deep into the young man's asshole yet again. The married man's face was wet with saliva as he feasted on the boy's hole, pulling it wide apart and probing the furry rosebud with his darting tongue.

While Sam dined on Ian's ass, Tom pushed Aaron's large, muscular legs apart and up toward his shoulders. The rookie's manhole was slippery with spit and Tom's fingers easily penetrated his muscle. His soft groans filled the dark room as four fingers slid within the boy's pussy. Tom bathed his balls with his tongue, holding each one and sucking it gently at first, then harder until the rookie's belly quivered and he groaned anew. Aaron's penis leaked a steady flow of cock snot, a long string of silvery sweetness that dripped from the tiny lips of his throbbing cock, making a large sticky pool on his furry belly. Tom supped and sucked the rookie's hole and cock, feeling the tight virgin muscle give way until his large fingers slid in and out with rapid ease. Aaron pulled around and took Tom's rigid pole into his mouth and swallowed it until his lips rested against the man's chrome ring. His eyes watered as Tom's cock stretched his mouth and filled his throat, his gag reflex coming in waves. Aaron looked over and saw Sam feeding Ian his thick penis, fucking his face with long deliberate strokes that buried his member deep into the rookie's mouth, flattening his nose into his thick nest of black pubes.

"Ok rook, breeding time," Sam hissed pulling his cock out and slapping it noisily against Ian's soggy anus. The boy's eyes closed as the man's thick penis penetrated his hole and slid fully inside resting the man's gut and heavy sack against Ian's round ass. "Goddamn, I love plowing probie pussy," Sam said as began a rhythmic pumping into Ian's shitter.

"Oh my fucking God," Ian shouted as the pounding continued.

Tom pulled his cock out of Aaron's mouth, gripped the boy's thick, hairy ankles and let the tips of his penis rub against the spent asshole. Tom rocked back and forth twice and then pressed forward until the thick head of his cock split Aaron's sphincter. Tom's ass was a blur as he pounded again and again, deeply into Aaron's boyhole, ignoring the cries of pain. He finally leaned forward and pressed his mouth tightly against Aaron's, smothering out the shouts with deep kisses. Tom fucked the boy until he emptied his nuts again inside the ruined hole, white semen leaking from the stretched anus. Aaron's arms were tight around Tom's neck, the young man's kisses were deep and hungry. Across the bed, Sam shouted and ejaculated his thick load into Ian's spent asshole before collapsing on the sweaty rookie. Ian turned his head toward Sam and felt the man's tongue slide inside his open mouth.

"You are smokin' hot, buddy. I love fucking a rookie's ass like yours so much. Goddamn you love getting pounded." With that, Sam slid down and began to lick and suck Ian's cum-filled hole while the rookie writhed and moaned.

"I'm gonna nutt," he gasped.

Sam flipped him over and gripped the young man's penis as it erupted blast after blast of thick semen into the married man's goateed mouth. When Aaron saw that, he felt his own orgasm explode and Tom's lapped the hot sperm up from his hairy belly and leaking dick. The men lay still on the king-sized bed, soft sounds of kisses and breathing filled the warm bedroom. Aaron lay his head on Tom's big hairy chest and listened to the man's heart beat strong against his ear.

"I kind of love laying here like this," Aaron whispered listening to Ian and Sam's soft kissing against his back. His ass was rubbing gently against his friend's. He reached over and let his hand slide down his butt to his legs and back up. Ian's hand found his and slid his fingers into Aaron's. Tom's large hand brushed against Aaron's face and kissed the rookie again, smiling at the sweaty face, tasting the mix of sperm and salt on his tongue.

"I kind of love it too, little buddy. Always have. You boys mean the world to me."

"You can fuck me any time you want, Tom." Aaron said.

Tom rested his nose against the rookie's nose. "You can count on it."

Ian stood under the shower and washed away the sex from the night before and let the water flow over his solid muscled body. He ran the bar of soap in his ass crack and dug his finger into the smooth knot of flesh, penetrating his muscle. He stood with legs apart, probing his prostate and washing out his ass, smiling as he thought of all the meat and spunk that had been up inside it in the past 24 hours. A cold breeze momentarily floated past and he turned around feeling strong arms slide around his waist and pull him backward.

"There you are. I missed you in the bed," Aaron said in a low morning purr. His face brushed close to Ian's, his morning stubble tickling his cheek and causing his dick to swell. "Wow, it doesn't take much to get your dong excited," Aaron added, sliding a soapy hand down and gripping his friend's penis.

"From the boner rubbing my ass right now, I'd say I'm not the only one," Ian said with a smile. He turned around and slid his arms around Aaron's waist and pulled the young man close, pressing their bellies together. Ian's hands gripped Aaron's meaty ass cheeks and pulled him close, kissing him deeply. Aaron's hands slid up to Ian's neck and tenderly rubbed the rookie's sandy curls, allowing his other hand to prob his friend's surprisingly open rosebud. Ian's mouth opened in a soft gasp as Aaron's fingers penetrated him, finding the spot that caused his dick to leak and harden even more.

"I could get used to waking up with you like this, buddy," Ian said into Aaron's ear.

"Me too, big guy. I think I'm kind of crazy about you," Aaron said, blue eyes shining in the warm humid air. Aaron pulled back with a wicked grin. "Hey, what did you think of Tom and the piss stuff yesterday? Was it sick or..?"

Ian smiled wide himself. "Yeah, real sick. And a fucking huge turn-on as well."

Aaron's brow rose. "You peed yet this morning?"

"Um yeah, but I could piss again," Ian said with a twinkle in his eye.

Aaron slid down the thick furry legs in front of him until his face was level with Ian's cock. The wide mushroom head dripped with spray from the shower, resting on his ample sack in a half-hard salute.

"You sure, pal?"

"Let me have it, buddy."

Ian relaxed his belly and sent a warm, clear stream of pale yellow onto the patch of red-brown curls on Aaron's chest, spraying on his nipples and down to his belly and then his furry crotch. Then Ian directed the tip of his penis toward Aaron's face. Aaron opened his mouth wide and felt the hot stream fill his mouth and bubble out, flowing down on his neck and chest. As the stream died, Aaron swallowed Ian's dick and began to suck it hungrily. In a minute, Ian was unloading his morning nut deep into his new friend's mouth. Ian thrust his thick cock deep into Aaron's mouth grunting softly.

"Fuck me, that was so hot," Ian whispered.

"You want to give it a go?"

Ian grinned and turned his ass to Aaron, pulling his meaty cheeks apart. Aaron gripped his cock and let his piss stream blast against Ian's pink hole and furry sack that hung low between his legs. Then the rookie spun around and sunk to his knees, opening his mouth wide as Aaron's golden stream filled his mouth with warm, bubbling piss that leaked from the corners of his mouth and onto his wide chest. Aaron's dick slid inside Ian's mouth and the young man sucked eagerly until Aaron's semen shot within. The boys washed off together and dressed, heading to the kitchen to fine Tom and Sam having coffee.

"Looks like you guys have had a good morning already," Sam said.

Tom and the rookies drove to the unit office with Sam driving behind. Jake started morning briefing promptly, with most of the crew yawning and trying to clear their heads from the night before. Ian looked over at Brandon and Jesse who for some reason were sitting far apart, frowns on both their faces. *Oh shit, something is up with the big meatheads* he thought. Normally they couldn't keep their hands out of each other's pants. He noticed Ben and Colton were similarly angry looking and sitting far apart themselves. *Something is definitely wrong in fantasyland.* He casually jabbed Aaron in the ribs and nodded with his head toward the sullen looking crewmates. Aaron's eyebrows raised up into his hair and he cut his eyes sideways to the Ian, shrugging his shoulders in agreement something was definitely not right.

"Ok, we are getting deployed out to the Deschutes National Forest on a move-up," Jake began. "Weather is definitely heating up and there may be dry lighting moving through the area and they want some crews prepositioned. We are heading over to the Two Bulls Lookout. We will man the lookout, go on patrols, and be ready to head directly to fires on initial attack as they pop. The lookout hasn't been manned yet this year, so it's going to need some light maintenance. It's going to be pretty tight quarters for all of us, but I have a feeling we can make do with sleeping on top of one another."

"Word!" Eric bellowed from the back of the crew hall. Chad and Bayard standing near him did a fist bump with one another, big grins filling their faces.

"It's about time. Some of us have hardly had any OT since fire school, not to mention any rookie ass," Bayard barked.

"Way to keep it professional, Bayard," Jake said with a scowl. But the twinkle in his eyes betrayed his real feelings. *It was high time he was back inside one of his brothers as well* he thought.

By 10:00 the crew pulled out of headquarters in four engines and headed east on Hwy 20 toward the Deschutes National Forest. The lookout was at the base of the Three Sisters, a stunning vista of three volcanic peaks snowcapped all year long. The area was a vibrant recreation area and also prone to human-caused fires along with the inevitable threat of lightning caused wildfires. Ian and Aaron sat in the back of the rig along with Jesse who had piled in with them at the last minute. Chad and Eric rode in front, Oakley sunglasses and ball caps clung to their heads as the engine roared along the two-lane mountain road. Ian could feel Aaron's leg pressed hard against his on the one side. Jesse looked morosely out the window on the other side. Ian slid his hand casually into Jesse's lap gripping his thigh, barely brushing the big rookie's crotch.

"What up, my bro?" Ian asked. Jesse looked down and started to push Ian's hand away but looked up at him instead with a weak smile.

"Aw, it's nothing. Bran and me got off on the wrong foot this morning, that's all," he said. He slid his big leg over against Ian's and gripped the rookie's thigh, rubbing his hand up and down. "Shit, this is exactly what got me in trouble with Brandon."

"What do you mean?" Ian asked, his fingers crawling toward the large mound in Jesse's lap.

"It's just stupid. The other night, Brandon and I stayed with Ben and Colton. Things got a little intense between me and Colton. I don't know why. We just hit it off good. I could tell it was bugging Brandon. Then yesterday after shift, I was putting gear away in the fire cache and I feel someone behind me and when I turn around, its Colton. He's got his pants down around his ankles and his cock is all hard and dripping. He pushes my pants down and just bends me over a pile of hose and slides inside my hole. Fuck, it hurt like hell. But he just has this thing. I would do anything he wanted. He was fucking the shit out of me. He pulls my face back and we are kissing pretty hard and all that while he is pounding me when I look over and Brandon is standing in the doorway with his mouth open. Ben is standing behind him with his arms folded. Ben just yelled something and left. Colton kept pumping into my butt until he shot his nut, then kissed me again and patted me on the ass. He pulled up his pants and left leaving me there with my ass hanging out, cum dripping down my legs, and Brandon boiling mad."

"Holy shit," Ian said. Aaron reached his arm around Ian's back and gripped Jesse's shoulder.

"Sorry, Jess," he said.

Eric turned around and lowered his Oakley shades and glared at Jesse. "You really are a stupid piece of shit, rookie," Eric snapped, his ice-blue eyes shining in the bright sunshine.

Jesse opened his mouth to complain, but just kept quiet and slumped against the door again. Ian saw a single tear slide from underneath his sunglasses and down his stubbled cheek. Ian slid his hand into Jesse's.

"In case you forgot, Colton is a fucking married man. It's not cool to be fucking around with his husband right there in front of him. Believe me, I know all about that. Me and Rick and Sam all know about trying to keep spouses happy. It's easier for us because we don't rub our partner's faces in our extra-curricular sex. We keep it on the DL even though our ladies aren't stupid. They all know we connect with one another," Eric said gruffly.

"Well, okay. Maybe Colton is a fucking married man but he sure as shit doesn't act like it as far as we rookies are concerned. He fucks us like crazy all the time, right in front of Ben. It's him you should be yelling at, not Jesse," Ian said with more forcefulness than he would have imagined. Eric looked at him with a dangerous stare then broke into a wide grin.

"Well fuck me, Rook. Look who just found his balls." Eric and Chad broke into loud laughter.

"You are going to have to tell that bitch to calm the fuck down," Chad said. "Next time he wants your ass, you just stick to your guns and say he sure as shit better have his husband's permission. And you're right, those two idiots need to get their shit together and figure out how they are gonna deal with all the fucking around here without being pissy little jealous bitches."

"Let us deal with those dickheads," Eric said reaching his large calloused hand over to fist-bump Jesse. "Don't go crying about it either. If you and Frodo are the real deal, then trust each other and know what happens here in the brotherhood is way different than going off trolling for some Craigslist piece of ass."

"I think he's the one who needs to be reminded of that," Jesse said.

"Just be a man and tell him. He will understand. We aren't a bunch of emo-haired, skinny jeans wearing fuck-sticks. We are mother-fucking Hart Mountain Hotshot men. You hear me," Eric added.

"Preach it, brother," Chad echoed. "Figure your shit out because I fully intend to fuck the ever-loving piss out of you. You feel me?"

"Yes sir," Jesse answered tugging on his dick as it swelled in his Nomex.

The lookout was a four-room ranch-style house: kitchen-living room, bunk room, bathroom, and equipment room. Attached to the house was a tall lookout tower that stood over fifty feet in the air over-looking the expansive green carpet of lodge pole pine and juniper that covered the land at the foot of the Three Sisters. The kitchen had a large industrial-sized 6-burner propane stove and a big center island with bar stools around it as well as a large old-fashioned yellow Formica-topped dining table. The living room had two large overstuffed sectional couch-es that had definitely seen better days. Three other LazEboy recliners filled the space in front of the fireplace. Ian and Aaron were surprised to see the ancient television in the corner had been replaced by a 60-inch flatscreen, bought and paid for by the Prineville Hotshot crew who often spent the most time manning the lookout. They had recently been de-ployed to Montana on a fire resulting in the need to bring over another crew to man the lookout.

The bathroom was large with three toilets and a large old-fashioned ceramic urinal set against one wall and three sinks on the oth-er. The back of the bathroom was a large tiled shower room with four regular shower heads and three overhead rainhead fixtures. The tile work in the shower was fresh and new, another project completed by the

Prineville shots. The bunk room consisted of ten sets of bunkbeds. The crew noted that the bucks were grouped together into sets of two or more. Ian smiled realizing there just might some other crews out there who didn't mind the intimate togetherness being on a hotshot crew afforded.

"Okay men. Get your gear stowed away. Figure out where you are going to bunk and let's make a plan for this afternoon's patrol and then dinner and all the rest." Ian and Aaron looked around and made a line toward a set of bunks near a corner of the room, only to have Chad and Eric grab their stuff and throw it on the floor with a laugh.

"You rookies need to all dogpile together in the middle. We'll get you over to our beds soon enough," Sam said.

"Oh you know it, brother," Bayard added dumping his gear along with Rick's on the bunks near the bathroom door. Eric and Chad took a set of bottom bunks with Jake on top. Tom and Sam found beds in another corner with Colton and Ben whose face seemed etched with a permanent scowl. The rookies set up their gear in the middle of the room. Ian and Aaron along with Jesse and a visibly angry Brandon. Jordan and Nick made up their bed and wandered off to look around outside. Two new faces also joined the group. Jarvis Washington was a tall, muscular black firefighter that had just recently rejoined Hart Mountain after a stint with a Washington crew. He was joined by a thin, solid looking American Indian firefighter named Big Farmer. Big had a long black braid down the back of his head. His smooth ruddy skin was covered with a large number of tattoos down his arms. Ian noticed he had a tribal tattoo across the small of his back on top of his ass crack when he bent over to finish making his bed. Ian also noticed the enormous bulge in Jarvis's pants as the man casually scratched his balls taking with Jake.

"You think they are like the rest of us?" Aaron whispered.

As Ian looked at Jarvis chatting with Jake, the big black man reached over and gripped Jake's protruding basket in his pants, planting a long kiss on the man's lips.

"I'm gonna take a guess and say, yep," Ian said wondering what it was going to be like being mounted by either one of these new veterans, his sphincter contracting as he considered it.

The afternoon light turned gold as the crew divided up and took off on patrol. Jake had ordered Jordan and Nick to stay behind and cook the evening meal for the men. The rest of the crew took off on patrol, scouting the area around Linton Lake over to Linton Meadow and back around to the area around Proxy Falls. When Ian and Aaron saw the beautiful falls and the cool pool of water at the base, they thought back to their afternoon with Tom and wished they could stop and wade into the cold water with the rest of the crew and get caught up in the intense group sex that was bound to happen.

"Man, the next time we patrol around here we have to plan to stop and take a swim," Ian said.

"And spend some quality time between each other's legs," Aaron added reaching over and rubbing his hand up Ian's leg to his full crotch. Ian reached over and gripped Aaron's face and pulled him over and planted a big kiss on the side of his scruffy face.

"I'm kind of falling for you, buddy," Ian said with a wide grin.

That evening, the full crew feasted on spaghetti and meat sauce, a big green salad, and garlic bread. Jordan and Nick made a name for themselves with the veterans, receiving a number of slaps on the ass and big kisses on the sides of their faces. Ian smiled watching Tom grab Jordan from behind and wrap his big arms around him, sliding a hand down inside Jordan's Nomex pants and groping his junk until the rookie's penis stood at attention, straining against the dark green fabric. Ian thought, *Jordan's ass is going to be full of Tom's fat cock before he knows it.* Around 9:00 PM. Aaron joined Nick, Jordan, and Brandon in a game of Texas Hold 'em. It appeared whatever was messed up between Brandon and Jesse was not worked out yet. Ian went outside, taking in the darkening blue sky filling up with a million stars. The clear air was still and sparkled with diamonds. The horizon was a bloody rim of crimson against the edges of the mountains that surrounded the lookout. Ian began to climb the stairs and made his way quickly up the twelve flights until he poked his head in the lookout. His eyes flew open as he took in the scene.

Chad's face was buried deep inside Eric's smooth ass. The veteran's ice-blue eyes were closed as Chad's nose and tongue continued to devour his hole. Eric's pants were in a pile on the floor. He still wore his boots and a t-shirt. He stroked his cock with one hand as he pulled his butt apart with the other to allow Chad's hungry mouth full access to his man cunt. Chad's face was wet as he probed and tongue-fucked Eric deep and hard. A long drop of precum dripped in a silvery rope from the tip of Eric's penis down toward the floor. Eric's big round balls were tight and rolling in his sack, framed with dark brown fur that was thick and curly. Chad pulled his dick back underneath this legs toward his mouth and sucked on the tip while he ate Eric's hole, bathing his balls with an expert tongue and hungry mouth. Ian slid his hand inside his pants and felt the tip of his penis slick with precum, his erection hard and throbbing against his hand.

"Fuck me, amigo," Eric hissed gripping the edge of the open window, his legs bent and spread wide.

Chad stood and pushed his pants down off his ample round ass, his cock straining against his belly. The treasure trail of black fur snaked down his tan belly toward a thick crop of pubes that framed his 8 inch penis. His mushroom head was wet and shining in the evening light. It was wide and flared. Eric groaned loudly as Chad penetrated the man's anus and continued to slide forward until his pubes rested flat against Eric's creamy round buttocks.

"Motherfucker. I never get tired of feeling you inside me," Eric said.

"I never get tired of filling up this tight shithole of yours. I love riding you, baby," Chad said in between thrusts. His balls banged loudly against Eric's sack, filling the air with smacking, sweaty sex.

Ian lost his balance momentarily and when he did, his boots make the softest of sounds on the stairs. Both men's faces turned toward him and glared.

"Get your ass up here rookie," Eric bellowed, grunting as Chad continued to plow his hole.

Ian gulped and climbed the rest of the way into the lookout. "Thought you'd spy on us, huh?" Chad said, his face glistening with sweat as he fucked Eric again and again.

"No...I didn't. Honestly."

"Get over here and suck my dick you little shit," Eric command-ed. "And I want you bare-assed naked while you do it." Ian walked quickly to the other side of the lookout, pulling his t-shirt over his head and dropping his pants. He hopped on one foot and then the other as he managed to get his boots off and then pushed his underwear to the floor.

"Suck it, Rookie," Eric ordered.

Ian's mouth opened and was filled with the married man's puls-ing cock, dripping with precum. The pearly snot filled his mouth and Ian sucked hungrily on his member. Ian reached out and gripped Eric's ass, pulling the man deeper and deeper into his mouth. Chad's hard thrusts pushed Eric's cock more and more into Ian's face. Ian pulled off mo-mentarily and sucked on Eric's large balls, bathing his sack in spit with his tongue before moving back to the man's rigid shaft. Ian could feel the large flared head swell as rope after rope of hot man magma bubbled inside his mouth. Ian gulped and spluttered and swallowed the thick seed that continued to flow, blast after blast in rich pearly spurts.

Eric pushed Ian to the window and pulled the rookie's ass open wide and began to eat it voraciously as Chad continued to mount him. Eric's tongue penetrated the Ian's ring and slid in and out of the boy's ass like a snake. Eric spit gobs of saliva into the rookie's anus and ate his hole until the boy's ass was dripping and soaked.

Chad pulled out of Eric's ass and entered Ian in one solid thrust that drove the air out of the rookie and made him bend over in pain. Chad's solid Latino cock banged hard against the boy's prostate and brought tears to his eyes for a moment. But then, the man's rhythm began to tease and pleasure his ass like he had never felt before. Eric dropped to his knees and took the boy's penis into his mouth and began to suck and nurse on him, stroking his shaft and milking his balls.

"I'm fucking cumming!" Chad shouted, leaning into Ian's ass deeper than ever and unloading his semen deep within the rookie's boyhole. The Mexican seed filled Ian's ass and began to leak from the sides, coating his thick, furry blond legs with a river of ranch dressing. Ian groaned and felt his orgasm explode, filling Eric's mouth with hot rookie sperm. The veteran skillfully swallowed every drop then rose to slide his semen-flavored tongue into Ian's mouth, kissing the boy deep and hard. Chad pulled the rookie's face to his and Ian felt the man's tongue slip inside. Ian's hands caressed both veteran's ass cheeks as they kissed him, his face wet and swollen with kisses.

"Been looking forward to that, Rookie," Chad said in his sweet, musical voice. "Fuck, you know how to take some dick."

"And how to suck one too," Eric said. "Not all these guys can take all my nut."

"That was a lot of sperm," Ian said breathlessly.

"Now you know why this man knocked his wife up with triplets," Chad said with a chuckle.

"So how many times you been fucked, Rook?" Eric asked, bending down for his underwear, his penis slowly leaking another string of semen.

"Um, not sure. Kind of lost count. I guess like six or seven times at least."

"You have a natural fuckable manhole," Chad said. "My dick just slid right in."

"It hurt pretty good," Ian said with a smile. "Your cock is huge."

"That's why I am always wanting it up my shitter," Eric added.

The veterans dressed and made their way down the stairs. Ian stood in the dark lookout, enjoying the feel of the evening breeze on his naked body. The sky was a diamond carpet, glittering into his big blue eyes as he held on to the window. He was startled as large arms slid around his waist and pulled him back against an obvious erection. A scratchy two-day old beard slid against Ian's cheek. A warm mouth gently touched his face as he spoke.

"That was fuckin' awesome watching you get plowed by those guys. Damn, Chad's dick is big." Jesse's hand slid down and gripped Ian's semi-hard penis and stroked it and his sack, bringing him back to full erection again.

"Should you be doing this? Aren't you and Brandon..?"

"We're good. He's just mad that I've been playing with Colton so much, with him being married and all that. Pretty funny, Eric is married and a dad and no one seems to care his cock is buried up in a hole half the time."

"Yeah, this whole thing is complicated." Ian said with a sigh. He felt Jesse's dick head rub against his crack. His pants were pushed down to his knees and his erection probed inside Ian's crack and lined up against the boy's tired hole.

"I've wanted to fuck you since that first morning I saw this great ass in the tent, all open and sticky from Tom pounding you all night," Jesse whispered as his large hands gripped Ian's butt and rubbed the cheeks and teased his fuzzy hole. Ian laid his head back against Jesse's face and spread his legs to let his fellow rookie penetrate him; first with a finger, and this with his cock. Ian lifted his leg up on the window ledge feeling all of Jesse's eight inches slide within him. As the blond rookie's furry belly rested against his ass, Ian turned his face and allowed Jesse's tongue to slip inside his mouth as the young man began to pump slowly in and out of his well-used pussy.

"Holy fuck, your ass is perfect to breed," Jesse said picking up the pace. Ian gripped the window sill and felt even more of Jesse's cock penetrate him, the large loose balls banging steadily against his own sack. Jesse pulled him over to an old couch in the corner and sat down with Ian in his lap. Jesse continued to plow Ian's hole, moving his shaft almost out of the boy's hole and then all the way inside again with a grunt. Ian's cock was leaking copious amount of precum as he stroked it riding Jesse's dick.

"Yeah, ride that dick, brother. Oh shit, you are gonna make me nutt," Jesse gasped. Ian pulled off the cock and slid to his knees with Jesse gripping his penis and sending a thick three-shot load of hot cum on his lips, nose, and chin. He wiped up the load on the tip of his cock and fed it to Ian, shoveling it into the rookie's open mouth. Ian stood and slid his boner into Jesse's mouth and pumped twice before unloading his own seed into Jesse's hungry mouth. Jesse pulled Ian's ass toward him, burying the boy's cock deep inside his mouth, cleaning it completely before he pulled back.

"Thanks buddy," Jesse said. "I needed to take a load off." His mouth closed on Ian's who tasted sweat and semen on Jesse's lips. "I am down for that any time you are. Brandon's got to try out that amazing ass of yours too. Damn."

Ian reached around and gripped Jesse's firm round ass. "Next time, I am going to plow that hole of yours buddy. I think I know why Colton is so crazy for it."

"You got it, dude." Jesse pulled up his pants and started down the stairs. Ian dressed and followed him down a few minutes later.

When Ian got down to the great room, most of the crew was watching "Shawshank Redemption" on the big screen television. Most of guys were sitting on the large old sectional couches in various states of undress. Tighty-whities seemed to be the underwear of choice, but some of the rookies wore boxer briefs and a couple of guys even had on loose fitting regular cotton boxers. Sam was laying on one couch with his arm draped around Nick, his thick fingers slid inside the rookie's boxers fondling his dick which now stuck out of the vent, tip glistening with precum. Nick's head was resting on Sam's shoulder enjoying the exploration of his crotch. Brandon was naked, his head in Jake's lap, sucking on the man's large penis while Jake ran his hands through the rookie's curls. Big Farmer had his face and tongue buried deep in Brandon's furry trench, eating his hobbit hole with relish. Jesse stood on the side with his hand in his boxer briefs. Ian figured he must have lost his pants the minute he came back inside. He seemed to be enjoying watching his boyfriend be molested and servicing the two veterans.

Jordan was bent over the back of one of the couches, Bayard's face was clamped on the thin rookie's ass eating deep and hard while he stroked his thick uncut cock. Aaron sat on Rick's lap, the red-haired veteran's penis buried deep inside the rookie's cunt. The large sack rolled and pressed against the boy's fur-covered butt cheeks as he fucked in and out of the straining hole. Aaron leaned back, kissing the man deeply as he rode the thick cock. Ian smiled and felt a twinge of jealously, but that was quickly interrupted by Eric's smooth face sliding against his, his calloused hands sliding inside Ian's pants and gripping his cock.

"You ready for round two, Rook. I think I need to breed you."

"Yes sir," Ian said, turning around and looking deep into those ice-blue eyes.

"Get out of these clothes."

Two minutes later, Ian was face down on Eric's bed, the man's cock buried deep within his gaping hole.

"Fuck me, rookie. How much nut do you have up inside here?" Eric said into his ear.

"Not enough, sir," Ian said with a grin, wincing slightly as the married man's dick pounded deep against his prostate. Eric's mostly smooth belly was slick with sweat. He fucked fast and hard, holding on to Ian's head, keeping a hand over the boy's mouth to stifle the loud groans he kept eliciting. Ian looked over and saw Bayard now skillfully plowing Jordan who was on his back, his legs spread wide and held high up near his head. Bayard fucked relentlessly as the rookie whimpered and groaned, his legs spreading wide, his eyes closed with arms wrapped tight around Bayard's strong shoulders. Interestingly, Aaron was eating Rick's big ass and lining up his cock, sliding it inside the veteran who lay on his belly, smile on his face, enjoying being energetically fucked by his rookie buddy.

As Eric continued to grind deeper and deeper into Ian's ass, the rookie smiled to see Colton bent over with Ben savagely pounding his large ass. Tom's cock-ring circled penis hammering in and out of the big blond man's mouth as Ben raped his hole. Ian thought, *Looks like those guys have figured out their differences and Colton is getting sorted out the way he will understand the best.* Ben pulled his dick out and exploded a huge wad of nut on Colton's ass crack, then mopped up the load and pushed it hard back into the blond furry hole, wet and pink with wear. Tom grunted hard and unloaded his own bull balls into Colton's stretched mouth, two thin streams of semen leaking out the sides of his gulping mouth. As soon as Tom pulled out, Chad took his place and slammed his burrito deep into Colton's mouth, thrusting deep and hard, knocking his furry belly against Colton's nose. Stepping up behind Ben, a glistening dark Jarvis moved Ben to the side and settled his ten inch cock against Colton's worn out manhole. Colton's eyes popped open and he yelled a guttural scream as Jarvis's horse cock found its way deep inside the man's cunt, mangling his prostate and opening his pussy wider and wider.

Eric leaned down and kissed the side of Ian's face as his triplet-powered sperm blasted into his sore rectum, running down his heavy sack and pooling between the rookies legs. "I love fucking you, Ian. You may be my favorite rookie."

Ian reached behind him and hugged Eric's head close, soaking in the manly love and companionship. *Goddamn,* he thought. *I love fucking around with these guys. I fucking love them.*

The crew shut off the lights and headed to their respective beds around 10:00. As Ian lay beside Aaron, feeling his friend naked and heavy beside him, snoring softly into his neck, wrapped up in each other's arms, he could hear other snores along with the muffled sounds of sucking, the sudden gasps or groans as a thick cock made its way inside an asshole, or the soft nuzzles of manly kisses. As he moved his crotch closer to Aaron's, the sleepy rookie grabbed his hairy leg under the knee and pulled it wide until Ian's penis slipped inside him. With a soft groan, Ian fucked him gently as they fell asleep with the rest of the crew lovingly doing the same.

The End

Here is a sample from another story you may enjoy:

The tall man shifted his weight to his right foot and stuck out his thumb. The wind ripped through his almost shoulder length black hair as well as the long worn-out overcoat he wore, sending the fabric behind him like dark wings. He wore sunglasses but the light wasn't bright. His long black coat swirled around his tall frame like a bullfighter's cape. Nathaniel stood on the side of Hwy 11 and peered up into the Brooks Range, shrouded in mist. The air was clear blue for now, but another storm was heading this way. He had walked for so long, part in this world, part in between. Sometimes he wanted to spend all his days in the in-between. It was empty, lonely, and suited his personality.

As he stood on the empty road, the ages ran through his mind. To a mortal mind, it would be inconceivable. To him, it was just a smattering of days. He had watched the Fall of Rome and the rise of the Renaissance. Normally from afar, through the long dark void that separated this world from his prison. Even from that distant vantage point, he watched mankind grow and change, rise and fall, ascend to the heavens and probe the depths of the oceans.

His mistake had always been one of love, or at least, loving the wrong one. The Prince of Light had promised him eternal love, eternal joy, and a chance to rule the world along his side. It just made so much sense when he said it. He never stopped loving the Creator of course, he was just blinded by the light and beauty and a chance to be even closer to the other object of his love: mankind, especially the female variety.

When the rebellion began, Nathaniel's heart was broken. He never signed on for that. His mentor had promised the Creator was in agreement. His wrath had been so vast. When the forces of the Creator broke through the fortress, it was as if Nathaniel had watched his heart being ripped away from him. Then the horrible moment when the legion was cast out, like his very soul had been pierced. As the dawn of his separation from the Creator opened, Nathaniel cried out in pain and loss, to be severed from that heavenly love was beyond cost, beyond bearing.

And yet, he had endured. When most of the legion transmogrified into Lucifer's host, Nathaniel and a handful other others kept true. If there was any way to return to the Creator, he would do so. He had spent eons now in that vast blank place, neither alive nor dead, but watching...watching.

When the radiance of Michael had penetrated the void that was his home, Nathaniel could not look upon him. So long it had been since he had used his eyes to gaze upon the divine. His own angelic traits had all but disappeared over the ages. With one touch of Michael's hand, his heart surged to life. That long-dead ember flared to life and nourished his emaciated soul. When Michael spoke, it was as if thunder and lightning flashed within him.

"Would you be restored to the Creator?" the voice like hundreds of waters said.

"Yes, my brother," Nathaniel.

"It is long since you were that," Michael intoned. "But you have kept your gaze on mankind and your love for them has not diminished. If you are willing, there is a way for you to once again ascend to the heavens."

"But say the word, brother, and I will obey," Nathaniel said still with his gaze down at the ground.

Michael's fiery hand touched his face and lifted his chin. The brilliance of his person burned away so much vile corruption. He felt unencumbered from chains of his own forging for the first time in centuries. The rainbow blade that hung at his waist was pulled forth and its tip was placed on Nathaniel's chest. Michael slid the blade within, a pain like no other shuddered through him. Then a balm, sweet and languid flowed through his being and shook him to the core. When the blade was withdrawn, his shrunken, husk of a heart beat in vibrant gallops in his chest.

With that, Michael slid his hand inside the riven chest and soon thrust his entire form within Nathaniel's. The Fallen shook and trembled, vibrating with power and love. The connection was brief, but it brought him back to life. He felt a love and passion grow within his belly and groin. His member swelled to life as Michael stirred within him and soon, a cascade of urgency erupted from him in a mighty flow.

As Nathaniel opened his ice-blue eyes, Michael stood before him again.

If you enjoyed this sample then look for **Rise From Abyss.**

Also by this Author:

The Hotshot Brotherhood

Brokeback Buddies

Drive My Engine, Rookie

South Patrol Pounding

Shower of Power

Rise From Abyss

From the Author

Check my blog for Updates and interesting info.

Author Blog - angus-macgregor.awesomeauthors.org

If you enjoyed any of my books then please share the love and click like on my books in Amazon.

If you write me a review and send me an email I will send you a free book, or many.
(Just know that these emails are filtered by my publisher.)

Good news is always welcome.

One Last Thing, For Kindle Readers...

When you turn the page, Kindle will give you the opportunity to rate this book and share your thoughts on Facebook and Twitter. If you enjoyed my writings, would you please take a few seconds to let your friends know about it? Because... when they enjoy they will be grateful to you and so will I.

Thank You!

Angus MacGregor
angus_macgregor@awesomeauthors.org

About the Author

Angus MacGregor resides with his family in Oregon and Hawaii. Along with his passion for writing, Angus enjoys growing orchids, snorkeling and hiking.

Angus has worked as a school teacher, a financial analyst, and a small business developer. He currently works as a writer and supports firefighting efforts by working on wildfires in the US during the summer months. In addition to his adult erotica books, Angus has recently completed his first book of mainstream fiction.

"I love seeing what the Universe has in store for me as I create this reality. I love my life and the blessings of all the people and gifts that surround me. I wish peace and blessings to all my readers."

www.ingramcontent.com/pod-product-compliance
Lightning Source LLC
Chambersburg PA
CBHW071348130626
46556CB00005B/2080